D0494988

700032489815

...utter Muttaburra

Caramel Carnivore

Apricot Croc

Sunshine Scutes

Wrong Meteorite

Extinct Pink

Brontosaurus Blush

Me Nodo...

Dynamo

Puce Paras...

Razzle Dazzle Raptor

T. Rex Tongue

Poppy Predator

Ruby Riojasaurus

Brilliant Bambiraptor

Splendid Spinosaur

Ginger Geology

Tomato Tricer...

Gold Coloradia

Red Bed Rock

Madder Mesozoic

...l Proposal

Big Yolk

Hot 'n' Drysaur

Vivid Volcano

Clashing Claws

Blond Duckbill

Choc Latte Tria...

Ruddy Osteoderm

True Blue Troodon

...omate Plates

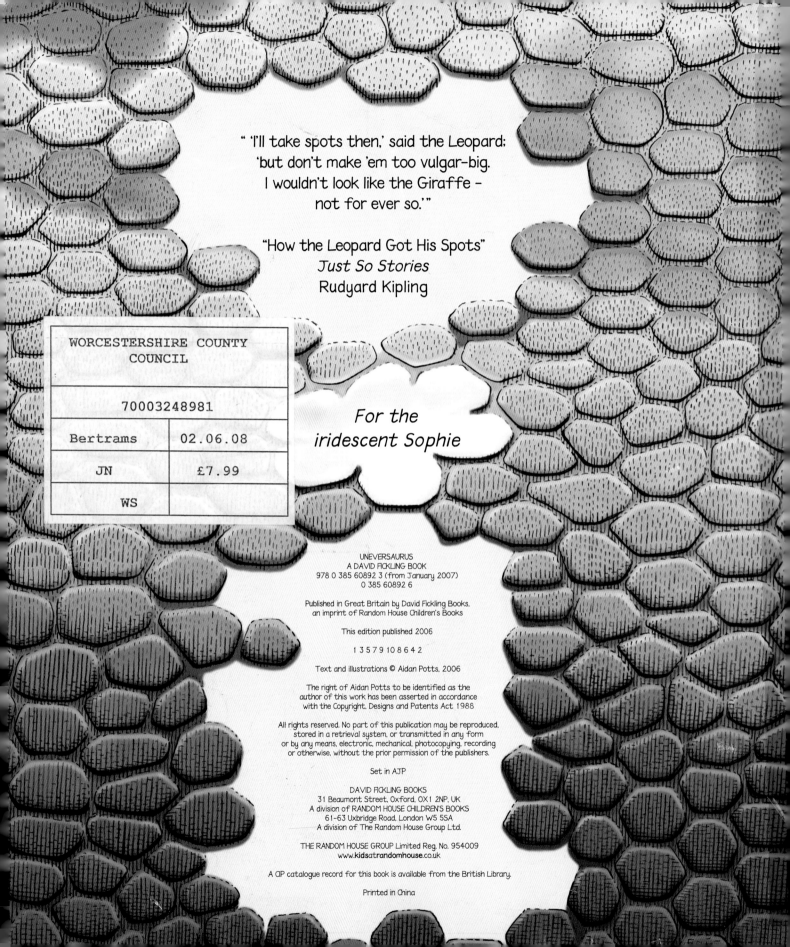

" 'I'll take spots then,' said the Leopard;
'but don't make 'em too vulgar-big.
I wouldn't look like the Giraffe –
not for ever so.' "

"How the Leopard Got His Spots"
Just So Stories
Rudyard Kipling

WORCESTERSHIRE COUNTY
COUNCIL

70003248981	
Bertrams	02.06.08
JN	£7.99
WS	

*For the
iridescent Sophie*

UNEVERSAURUS
A DAVID FICKLING BOOK
978 0 385 60892 3 (from January 2007)
0 385 60892 6

Published in Great Britain by David Fickling Books,
an imprint of Random House Children's Books

This edition published 2006

1 3 5 7 9 10 8 6 4 2

Text and illustrations © Aidan Potts, 2006

The right of Aidan Potts to be identified as the
author of this work has been asserted in accordance
with the Copyright, Designs and Patents Act 1988

All rights reserved. No part of this publication may be reproduced,
stored in a retrieval system, or transmitted in any form
or by any means, electronic, mechanical, photocopying, recording
or otherwise, without the prior permission of the publishers.

Set in AJP

DAVID FICKLING BOOKS
31 Beaumont Street, Oxford, OX1 2NP, UK
A division of RANDOM HOUSE CHILDREN'S BOOKS
61-63 Uxbridge Road, London W5 5SA
A division of The Random House Group Ltd.

THE RANDOM HOUSE GROUP Limited Reg. No. 954009
www.kidsatrandomhouse.co.uk

A CIP catalogue record for this book is available from the British Library.

Printed in China

UNEVERSAURUS

Professor Potts

by
Professor Potts

d·b FICKLING

David Fickling Books

No human has ever seen a dinosaur.

SO HOW DO WE KNOW WHAT THEY LOOKED LIKE?

Dinosaurs are buried treasure.

Their bodies have been fossilized, turned into stone. The fossils are only found in rocks that are between 65 and 230 million years old. They are worth millions of pounds.

EARLY JURASSIC TO LATE TRIASSIC SEDIMENTARY ROCKS

EARLY JURASSIC BASALT

MIDDLE TO EARLY PALEOZOIC

EARLY PALEOZOIC AND PROTEROZOIC

PROTEROZOIC AND MIDDLE PALEOZOIC

STRATIGRAPHIC MAP

QUATERNARY

TERTIARY

CRETACEOUS

JURASSIC

TRIASSIC

CAMBRIAN

PRECAMBRIAN

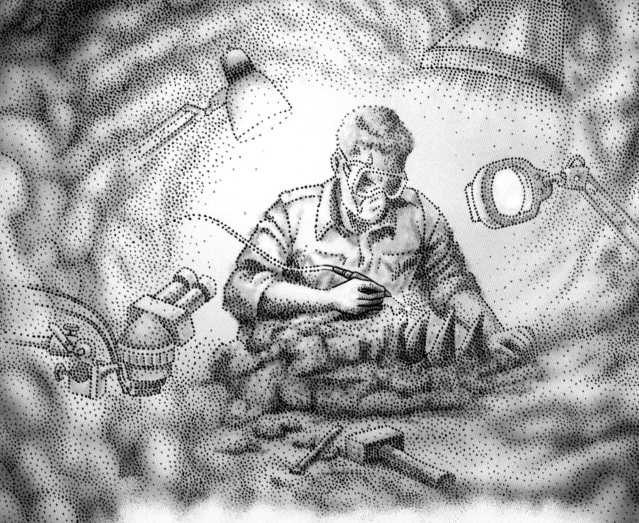

The fossils are **very fragile.**

They have to be dug up, transported and cleaned with great care.

It takes hundreds of thousands of hours to clean a big skeleton.

When bones are found

they're often jumbled up.

Some bones are broken and need fixing.

Some bits are missing and need replacing.

So, what did dinosaur skin look like?

Some dinosaurs had hard scales or bony plates and some had feathers.

One thing we can be sure of: no dinosaurs had long fur.

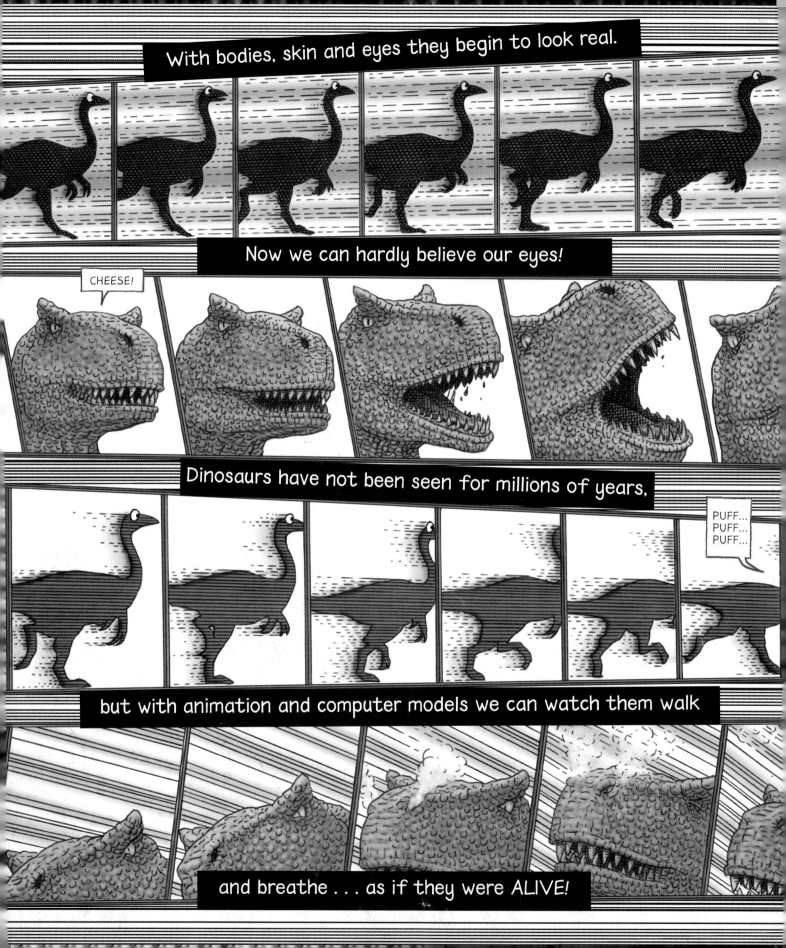

A very common type of camouflage is "countershading".

Light and shadow make things appear round, solid and easy to see.

Many creatures have a light colour where there is shadow and a dark colour where there is strong light.

In a way this cancels out the light from the sun.

It helps the animals to hide by looking flatter.

BERT'S SOLID GONE!

Disruptive colour also helps animals to hide in herds. The patterns mix the creatures together. Some dinosaurs might have been lost in a crowd.

What kind of world did the dinosaurs hide in? It was warmer, with no seasons. There was less snow so dinosaurs probably weren't all white.

We know from plant fossils that grass was rare, so camouflage like tiger stripes wouldn't have worked.

Hide your eyes!

Because eyes are easy to spot.

Some creatures have a dark cap or stripe.

Some reptiles can narrow their pupils into a thin slit.

U.C?

I.C!

Some creatures are bright, bold and flashy.

They use colour to surprise or scare
predators. Large eyespots
give a small animal
a giant stare.

Colour can sometimes be used as a warning. Creatures can look unappetizing. This is called aposematism.

FOOD IS NOT BLUE!

There are so
many amazing colours
around us.

Did dinosaurs blush, just like us? It would help their bodies cool down.
It might also be a sign that says "Watch out! I'm getting A-N-G-R-Y!!!"
Red is for danger!

ADULT.

Some of today's reptiles can transform!
They change colour as they grow by shedding skin.
If dinosaurs were able to do this we need to give
them at least two different coloured skins.

JUVENILE.

Dinosaurs were often gigantic,
BUT what colour is
BIG?

The largest
land animals
on earth
today are
simple light
colours.

They have few enemies,
they are too big to hide.
A light colour helps
a big animal stay
cool inside.

ELEPHANT HUES!

I MATCH THE SKY!!

Girls and boys are different.
Did Mademoiselle Dinosaur need to be dull brown to hide in her nest on the ground? Or did she wear princess pink to turn the boys' heads?

Reptiles and birds see more colour than we do. They can see ultra-violet. So dinosaurs might have been covered in UV markings, which human beings wouldn't be able to see.

What dinosaurs ate is important.
Some animals become the same
colour as their food. Flamingos are
pink because their food has
a lot of red dye in it.

YOU ARE WHAT
YOU EAT!

TOO MUCH
BUBBLE GUM!

If a dinosaur ate raspberry
ripple ice cream
would it become
pink and white?

The truth is not even the experts know what colour dinosaurs were. So we have to be creative.

THAT'S MEGA!

GIGA IS BIGGER!

SPOT THE DINOSAUR!

Tyrannosaurus Rex

Pteranodon (flying reptiles)

Hairy Triceratops

Stegosaurus

Archaeopteryx

Sleeping Spinosaur

Grey Brachiosaurus
Brown Diplodocus

On the left: Diplodocus
On the right: Brachiosaur

Chasmosaurus

Clockwise from top centre:
Corythosaurus
Tsintaosaurus
Lambeosaurus
Parasaurolophus
Saurolophus
Pachycephalosaurus

Protoceratops

Torosaurus

Carnotaurus